Strawberry Shortcake
Sleeps Over

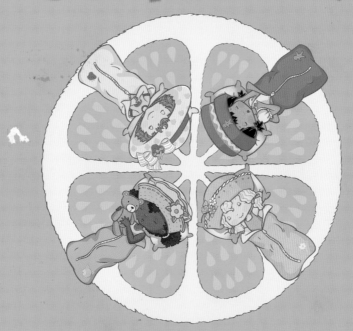

By Siobhan Ciminera

Illustrated by SI Artists

GROSSET & DUNLAP • NEW YORK

Published by Grosset & Dunlap, a division of Penguin Young Readers Group, 345 Hudson Street, New York, New York 10014.
GROSSET & DUNLAP is a trademark of Penguin Group (USA) Inc. Manufactured in China.

ISBN 0-448-43516-0
1 3 5 7 9 10 8 6 4 2

Orange Blossom was berry excited—it was the night of her big sleepover party! She had been planning it for weeks.

"Let's see," Orange Blossom said to her pet butterfly, Marmalade, as she checked her list. "We cleaned the house and made the food. We planned all of the activities for the party. Now all that's left is decorating!"

Just then, the doorbell rang. It was Strawberry Shortcake.

"Hi, Strawberry!" Orange Blossom said, looking at the clock. "You're early! The party doesn't start for another hour."

"I'm sorry, Orange," Strawberry said. "I was so excited about your party, I just couldn't wait."

"That's okay," said Orange. "Would you like to help me put up the decorations?"

"Sure!" replied Strawberry Shortcake. "Look at all these pretty balloons and streamers!"

Put a jewel sticker on your favorite decoration.

At five o'clock, Angel Cake and Ginger Snap arrived, right on time.
"Yay! Everybody's here! Now the party can start!"
Orange Blossom said excitedly. "Would you like some
fresh-squeezed orange juice? I made it myself!"

Add a jewel sticker to the scene.

"No!" Orange interrupted. "This is *my* sleepover and *I* want to read a story!"
"Fine," said Angel. "Then *I'm* going home." She stormed out of Orange
Blossom's tree house, slamming the door behind her.

Orange Blossom sat down and started to cry. "I just wanted to have a fun sleepover party for my friends!" she sobbed. "Now Angel Cake is mad at me!"

Give Orange Blossom a jewel sticker to make her feel better.

Strawberry Shortcake put her arm around Orange.

"Don't cry, Orange," Strawberry said kindly. "Angel's not mad at you—her feelings were hurt because she thought you didn't like her idea. But parties can be even more fun when friends take turns doing their favorite things."

Orange Blossom thought for a moment. "You're right, Strawberry," she finally said. "I didn't mean to be so bossy. I wish Angel Cake was still here so I could tell her that myself."

Then Orange Blossom had an idea. "I know!" she exclaimed.
"I can go to Angel's house right now and tell her I'm sorry!"

"Berry good idea!" said Strawberry
Shortcake. "Let's all go!"

"And we can bring her back to the
party," added Ginger Snap.

Strawberry, Ginger, and Orange
grabbed flashlights and jackets. Before
they walked outside, Orange Blossom
turned to her friends and said, "I feel
so much better now. Thanks!"

Give Strawberry Shortcake and
Ginger Snap a jewel sticker each
for making their friend feel better.

A full moon brightened the night sky, and the girls didn't need their flashlights to find their way to Angel Cake's house.

"Let's play flashlight tag!" Ginger Snap suggested on the way to Cakewalk.

Add a jewel sticker to the beautiful night sky.

"Berry cool," replied Strawberry Shortcake. "Not it!"

"Not it!" returned Ginger. "Looks like you'll have to come get us, Orange!"

The girls giggled as they raced down the Berry Trail.

A few minutes later, the friends arrived at Angel Cake's house. Orange Blossom shyly knocked on the door.

Angel Cake looked surprised to see her. "Hi," she said quietly.

"Hi, Angel," replied Orange. She took a deep breath. "Angel, I'm so sorry I was bossy at my party. I didn't mean to hurt your feelings."

"Thanks, Orange," said Angel with a smile. "I'm sorry, too. I feel so silly for getting mad and running out of your party. Can we start over?"

"Absolutely!" exclaimed Orange Blossom, giving her friend a hug.

Give Orange Blossom and Angel Cake jewel stickers for apologizing to each other.

On the way to her tree house, Orange Blossom turned to Angel Cake and said, "When we get back, let's make some friendship bracelets."

"Or we could listen to a story," Angel quickly replied.

"Wait a minute," Strawberry Shortcake interrupted. "Let's make friendship bracelets and listen to a story at the same time!"

"Berry good idea," said Ginger Snap. "Let's race! On your mark, get set, go!"

Decorate the scene with some jewel stickers.

When the girls returned to Orange Blossom Acres, they changed into their pajamas and took turns telling funny stories. The four friends laughed and laughed while they made pretty friendship bracelets.

After she finished telling her story, Orange Blossom turned to Angel Cake and handed her a beautiful friendship bracelet with pink and purple beads. "I made this for you, Angel," Orange said. "I'm so glad we're friends, and that you came to my sleepover party!"

"And I made this for you!" Angel Cake handed Orange Blossom a bracelet with red and orange beads. "I'm glad we're friends, too. Thanks for having such a great party!"

Help Orange and Angel finish their friendship bracelets by adding some jewel stickers.

"I think it's time to go to bed now," Orange Blossom said with a yawn. "Look, Ginger Snap is already asleep!"

The girls giggled quietly.

"I'm tired, too," whispered Angel Cake. "Good night, everybody! I had a great time."

"So did I!" added Strawberry Shortcake as she turned out the light. "Berry sweet dreams, Angel and Orange!"

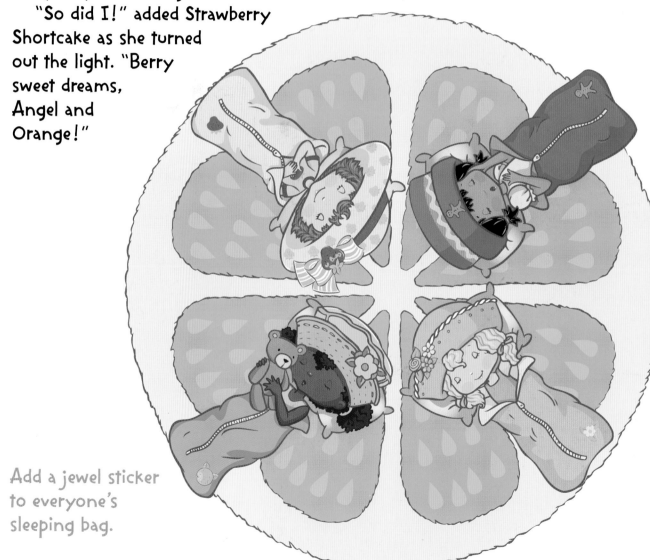

Add a jewel sticker to everyone's sleeping bag.